THOMAS & FRIENDS™

BIG WORLD! BIG ADVENTURES! THE MOVIE™

THE MOVIE STORYBOOK

EGMONT
We bring stories to life

First published in Great Britain in 2018 by Egmont UK Limited,
The Yellow Building, 1 Nicholas Road, London W11 4AN

Thomas the Tank Engine & Friends ™

CREATED BY BRITT ALLCROFT

Based on The Railway Series by The Reverend W Awdry
© 2018 Gullane (Thomas) LLC.
Thomas the Tank Engine & Friends and Thomas & Friends
are trademarks of Gullane (Thomas) Limited.
© 2018 HIT Entertainment Limited. HIT and the HIT logo are
trademarks of HIT Entertainment Limited.
All rights reserved.

ISBN 978 1 4052 9167 5
68250/001

Printed in EU

Egmont takes its responsibility to the planet and its inhabitants
very seriously. We aim to use papers from well-managed forests
run by responsible suppliers.

CHAPTER 1

One sunny morning, Thomas is puffing around the Island of Sodor when he sees a little yellow racing car flying around the bends beside the tracks.

"Hello!" peeps Thomas. "Want to race?"

"**Race?!**" replies the car, cheekily. "What, a little racing car like me against a **BIG** tank engine like you? **Alright mate! Ready – Set –**"

Thomas races off before he can say 'Go!', but the racing car is toying with him and he speeds ahead, leaving Thomas struggling to catch up.

Ace arrives at Ffarquhar Station first.

"**That was amazing!**" squeals Thomas. "Who are you?"

"My name's Ace!" laughs the little racing car. "**And I'm on a race round the world!** Five cross-country rallies on five different continents - Africa, South America, North America, Asia and Europe! I'm here to catch a ship to the first race."

"**Oh wow!** That's so exciting!" replies Thomas. "I've always wanted to see the world!"

"Then why don't you?" smiles Ace. "**You could be the first railway engine to go all the way around the world!**"

With that, Ace kicks up the dust as he races away, leaving Thomas imagining the possibilities.

Thomas hurries along the line to Knapford Station. He is impatient to ask The Fat Controller a question.

"Sir, how would you like it if one of your engines could be the first railway engine to go right round the world?"

"Around the world?!" smiles an amused Fat Controller. "I've never heard of a railway engine going around the world ..."

"I know, sir! It's never been done before!" replies Thomas.

"Well, Thomas, it would be marvellous if it could be done, but **the world's not all one big railway,** you know ..." begins The Fat Controller before he is interrupted by his phone ringing.

The Fat Controller comes out of his office to discover that Thomas is **missing**! The engines search around Sodor for him, but he is nowhere to be found.

A few days later, in the city of Dakar on the West Coast of Africa, Thomas has been lowered from a ship onto the tracks.

"**Welcome to Dakar, Thomas!**" cries Ace. "What do you think?"

"**Wow, Ace! I love it,**" peeps Thomas. "The ships, the people, the sounds, the smells ... everything! I'm so glad you invited me to come with you!"

Ace and Thomas set off into the Sahara where they meet the other racing cars.

"**I'm Thomas and I'm coming with you!**" peeps the little engine excitedly, but the racing cars are very surprised.

"**You?! How can a railway engine cross the desert?!**" they laugh.

"Ace invited me," replies Thomas.

"No, I didn't," says Ace, blushing. "**Why would I say you could come with me when there aren't any tracks?!**"

Thomas' face falls as all the cars take off to Dar es Salaam, leaving him behind and unable to follow.

CHAPTER 2

In the Shunting Yard, Thomas has been mistaken for a new engine they were expecting to pull some trucks to Dar es Salaam in Africa. The Yard Manager is unhappy about how little Thomas is and doesn't think he'll be up to the job, but Thomas is sure he can rise to the challenge.

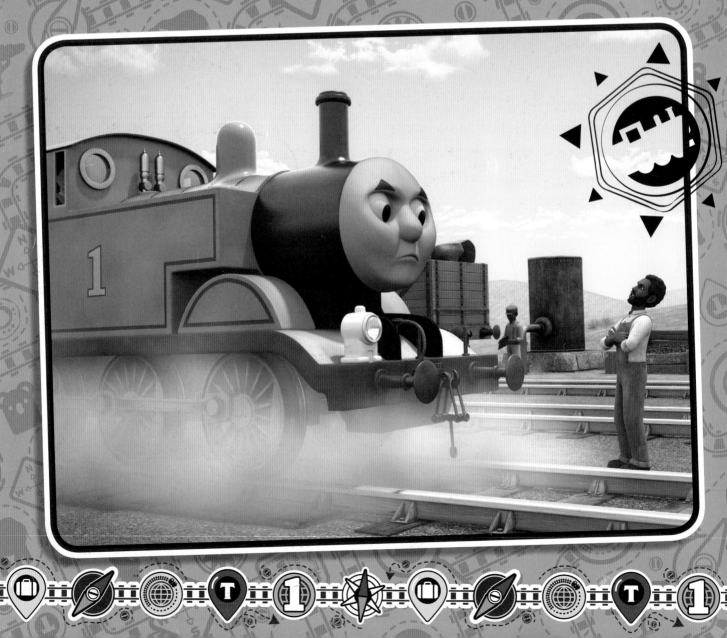

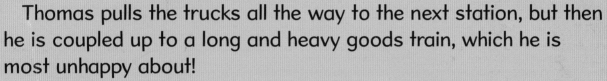

Thomas pulls the trucks all the way to the next station, but then he is coupled up to a long and heavy goods train, which he is most unhappy about!

"**Hee, hee, hee! Your face!**" laughs Nia, a tank engine from Kenya. "There are always a lot of trucks for Dar es Salaam, but usually they send a bigger engine. **I can help you.**"

"**I don't need any help!**" peeps Thomas, defiantly.

But, when the track goes up a hill, Thomas starts to struggle and his wheels spin under the weight of the trucks.

"**Whooooaaa!**" Thomas' brakes can't hold on any longer, and he starts sliding back down the hill.

Luckily, someone stops him from falling just in time - it's Nia!

"What did I tell you, Mister Blue Tank Engine?" she cries. "I knew you'd need help!"

"I DON'T NEED HELP!" calls Thomas. But as soon as she lets go, he starts to fall back. **Aarghh!"**

Nia pushes Thomas forward again. "Should I call you Mister Blue Tank Engine? Or do you have a name?" she asks. **"My name is Nia."**

Thomas is over the top of the hill now and feels a bit more confident. "I'm called Thomas ... and I can pull this train **BY MYSELF!"** he shouts as he races down the hill. **"Goodbye, Nia!"**

However, it isn't long before Nia is right behind him once more.

"If you want to go faster you should let me help you," she says. "After all, it's 5000 miles to Dar es Salaam!"

"**5000 miles?!?!**" replies a very surprised Thomas.

The trucks and Nia sing cheerily to lift his mood.

"Wake up! There's a world to see. Things to discover and try. Wake up! It's all around you now. As big as the beautiful sky."

As they look out over the savannah with giraffes running alongside them, Thomas is laughing and singing along too. This is what he has always wanted. He is finally seeing the world.

"Africa is a **wonderful** country," he smiles back at Nia.

"Africa is not a country, Thomas!" Nia laughs. "Africa is a continent. **We've passed through many different countries already** ... and we'll pass through even more before we reach Dar es Salaam in Tanzania!"

Meanwhile, in the port of Dakar, The Fat Controller has just arrived. After a thorough search of Sodor, he discovered that Thomas was loaded onto a ship to Africa and he's here to bring him back home safely.

"**Have you seen a little blue tank engine?**" he asks the locals. "He was following some racing cars …"

"Ah, they went into the Sahara," replies a camel herder.

"**The desert?!**" cries The Fat Controller. "Is there even a railway track through the Saha-?"

But, before he can finish his question, the camel steals his hat and begins eating it!

"You must forgive Ijin," says the camel herder. "He loves to try new foods."

Thomas and Nia have now arrived in the busy port of Dar es Salaam. The trucks are happy to be home.

"Ok, everybody!" peeps Thomas. **"Now you need to keep your eyes open for my friend, Ace."**

Nia is confused. "Who's Ace? **I thought you wanted to do everything by yourself!"**

Just as Thomas is about to explain about the race, Nia sees her friend Kwaku, a huge Garratt engine.

"Nia, how are you?" he asks, smiling warmly. **"Have you found a new engine shed where you can live yet?"**

Nia replies politely, but Thomas interrupts their conversation, only to discover that Ace has left Dar es Salaam without him.

"You might as well go home, Nia," he snaps. "I'll go to Rio by myself!"

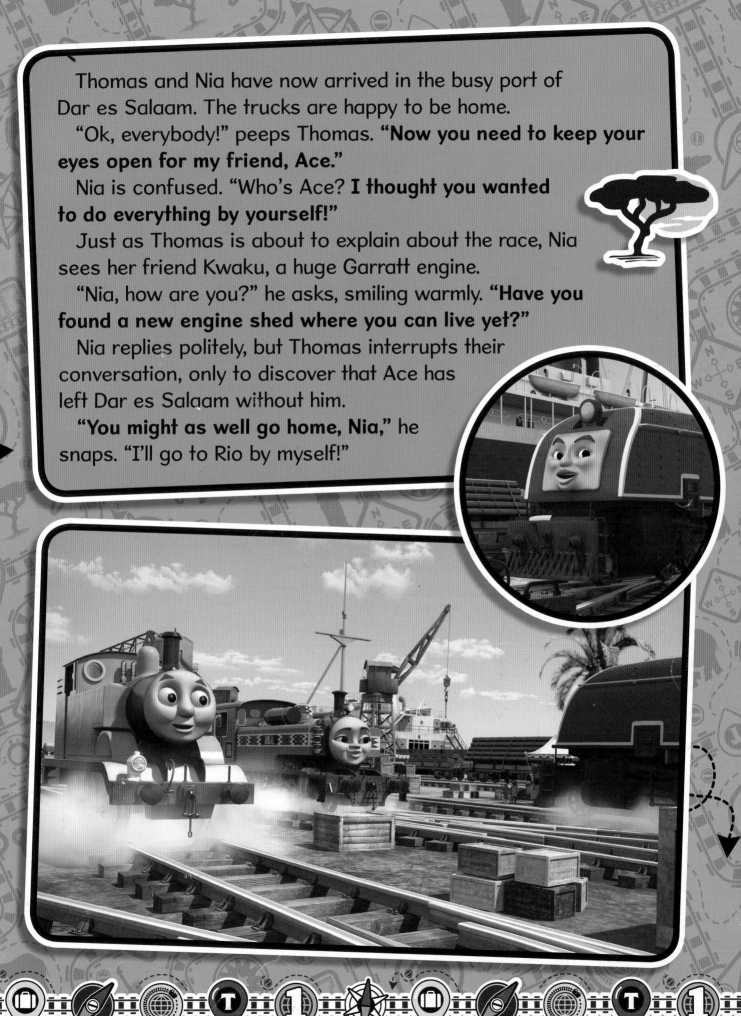

CHAPTER 3

Thomas is feeling sad and nervous as he is lowered onto another ship surrounded by crates and no friendly faces. But then he hears a familiar voice. **"Hey, hey, Thomas!"** It's Nia! "I'm coming with you to see the world too!" she says.

Thomas is shocked and surprised. **"What?!** Ace said I was going to be the first railway engine to go around the world!"

"Then I can be the second," replies Nia. **"Where is Ace?** Why isn't he helping you?"

"Because ... I don't need any help!" scowls Thomas.

"Everybody needs help," smiles Nia, before she falls asleep.

Suddenly Thomas spots a familiar racing stripe. He doesn't have to go to Rio to find Ace as he's on board the same ship!

"G'day, mate! Glad you could make it!" says Ace, cheerfully.

"Ace! I didn't know where you'd gone!" replies Thomas.

"That's the best way. Free and easy!" laughs Ace. **"You don't need any baggage to tie you down.** Good night, mate."

And they both shut their eyes and fall asleep.

Thomas is woken by bright carnival music.

"We're in Rio de Janeiro, Thomas," cries Nia. **"Brazil!"**

"Continent number 2, Thomas! South America," shouts Ace. "The next race is through the Amazon!" and with that he's off.

Thomas is impatient to follow him, but he'll need to agree to carry more cargo first.

"If you take this coffee to San Francisco, you can fill up with all the coal and water you need!" says a Railway Worker.

Thomas agrees and is surprised as Nia pulls up beside him. **"We can take it together,"** she peeps happily.

Thomas is disappointed that he isn't going with Ace instead.

BRAZIL

As they travel through the hills and open countryside, Nia and the coffee trucks begin to sing again.

"We're friends! We're friends! That's what we are. We're friends! And if we're not friends yet, then we could be and I bet, you and I will get to be friends in the end!"

Thomas is grumpy as they make their way into the Amazon.

"Maybe we should stop for water soon, Thomas," peeps Nia. "I have extra tanks, but you must be running low by now."

Thomas is about to reply when Ace races past, crying, **"Hey, Thomas! Look at me!"**

Thomas is so happy to see Ace that he races along after him, straight past the water tower.

Meanwhile, The Fat Controller is riding a camel across the Sahara Desert with a turban in place of his usual hat.

"Are you sure Thomas actually came this way?" he asks the camel herder. "There aren't any tracks here."

In the Amazon rainforest, Thomas and Nia are racing through pouring rain.

"I feel like a speedboat," peeps Thomas, happily. But as they splash along the flooded track, Thomas sees Ace lying on his roof.

"Ace! What happened?!" he cries.

"One of the hazards of rallying," chuckles Ace. **"I need help to get out of here and get to the Salt Flats in Utah to be repaired."** The jungle sounds are making him uneasy and even a little monkey frightens him!

Thomas and Nia set off through the rainforest again, with Ace loaded on top of the coffee sacks, when Thomas suddenly begins to slow down.

"Sorry ... but my boiler ... **it's run dry!**"

"We need to keep going!" says Ace, anxiously.

"But we can't go anywhere if Thomas doesn't have water. And I'm going to need water soon too," replies Nia. **"Maybe we can use leaves!"**

"LEAVES?!" say Thomas and Ace in surprise.

But Nia has the brilliant idea of using the large rainforest leaves to funnel rainwater into their tanks and soon they are full again.

"Wow, Nia. That worked a treat!" cries Thomas, peeping happily. "To the Salt Flats!"

The Fat Controller has somehow managed to make it safely to Dar es Salaam and is busy showing his picture of Thomas to everyone he meets.

"Yes. I've seen that tank engine," replies a crane. "I loaded him onto a ship heading for Rio De Janeiro in Brazil."

"B ... b ... Brazil?" asks The Fat Controller, losing his turban and finding it quickly replaced by a kofia hat!

In the Amazon, it is still raining heavily and the tracks are starting to sink under the weight of the trains.

"**Hurry, Thomas!** We must find solid ground or we'll get stuck!" cries Nia. "**Full steam ahead! One, two, three!**"

With that, Thomas and Nia both go full throttle, but as they race on over the bridge, the bridge support is washed away, leaving the track dangling over the water!

"**Oh no! Nia! Hurry!**" gasps Thomas and with one big push, the last coffee trucks clear the bridge, just as the tracks collapse into the rushing waters below.

"**Yes, we made it!**" cries Nia. "**We're a good team, aren't we, Thomas?**"

Thomas smiles happily, as Ace rolls his eyes.

Nia and Thomas steam on cheerily up through Central America towards Mexico.

Ace is in his element, singing along with the coffee trucks,

"Free - Free and easy! Set me on the road again.
Let me feel my tyres spin. Give me freedom that's a must.
I'm going to leave you in the dust!"

The trucks rock in time to the music, but Thomas is confused and Nia is more unsure of Ace than ever.

In Rio de Janeiro, The Fat Controller is showing his picture of Thomas to a diesel shunter.

"Yes, yes, I saw this engine. He was the one taking the coffee to San Francisco," replies the shunter.

"San Francisco?!" exclaims The Fat Controller, but then he spots a picture of a small propeller plane which gives him an idea.

Meanwhile, Thomas, Nia and Ace have now reached the USA and are travelling through Arizona in the southwest.

"Okay guys, you need to take me straight to the Utah Salt Flats!" says Ace. "That's where the next rally's going to be held: **North America. Continent number 3!**"

"But we're being useful, Ace. People are waiting for this coffee!" replies Nia. "The Salt Flats are **NOT** on our way.

"I'll tell you something that's even more important than being useful: having fun! Isn't that right, Thomas?" cries Ace.

Thomas wants to keep the peace and he smiles, but Nia is hurt. **"I know how to have fun too, you know!"** she says, letting her brakes off and sending Thomas backwards down the track.

Thomas and Nia almost hit another engine, but they miss it just in time and they giggle as they pull the trucks back up the slope. Ace is now feeling jealous of their friendship.

They continue their journey through Arizona, but Ace thinks they should split the train in two and pull their own half.

"But we're all going to San Francisco," says a shocked Nia.

"The coffee would definitely get delivered on time if you were racing, Nia!" replies Ace, trying to charm her. **"Unless you're worried that you can't keep up with Thomas?!"**

Nia rises to the bait, and soon the trains are uncoupled and the trucks are rearranged. They start to race along the line, side by side and neck and neck. But as they pass the signal box, Ace shouts to Thomas' Driver to turn off to the Salt Flats and the train plunges into a canyon at great speed!

"Aaarrrggghhh!" cries Thomas, as he sees an old Western mining engine up ahead, but luckily the startled engine moves into a siding just in time to clear the track.

Thomas slams on his brakes as hard as he can, coming to a stop just in front of a bend in the track. But the mining trucks are hurtling towards them, sending Thomas racing faster and faster, until he ends up on his side at the base of the canyon!

"**Wow, Thomas!**" chuckles Ace. "**What a ride!**"

"**We should have stayed with Nia,**" replies Thomas, sadly.

"Well, would you look at you?" says the mining engine. "No wonder you're lying in the dust, cowboy. This is **NOT** the wild west anymore! There's a speed limit for a reason."

"Yes, I know," replies Thomas. "We were going too fast. But someone needs to fetch the breakdown crane."

"**Breakdown crane?!** We use people power and horse power around here," laughs the old mining engine, chuffing away and leaving Thomas and Ace lying in the sand.

CHAPTER 5

The Fat Controller is flying overhead in Emerson, the small propeller plane, looking for Thomas, but it's much harder to see a little tank engine from that height than he thought.

Thomas and Ace have been in the desert all night and now the sun is blazing down on them.

"Thomas? Do they have wild animals here?" whispers Ace, uneasily, just as something lassoes Thomas' funnel.

"**A snake?!**" Ace gulps as a shadow falls over him, but Thomas can see horse hooves and cowboy boots beside him.

"**Ha ha, it's horse power, Ace!**" laughs Thomas. "And people power! Help has arrived!"

Soon Thomas and the coffee trucks are hauled back onto the tracks by a team of horses and cowboys. Then Ace is lifted up and repositioned on top of the coffee sacks!

"**Bust my buffers! Oh, thank you. That was amazing!**" peeps Thomas gratefully, as he chuffs away.

"**Happy trails!**" cries the old mining engine and the cowboys as they wave goodbye.

The Fat Controller has now reached San Francisco, and is speaking to a friendly diesel shunter called Amy.

"**He's blue, with a big number 1 ...** perhaps you've seen him?" he says. "Delivering coffee from Brazil?"

"**From Brazil?!**" Amy's face lights up. "Yes of course! I know the tank engine that brought the coffee, but she didn't look like that tank engine. Sorry."

The Fat Controller sighs, "**Oh, Thomas. Where are you?**"

Meanwhile, Thomas and Ace have arrived in the Utah Salt Flats. Ace is excited to be with the other racing cars, but Thomas feels really bad about losing Nia.

"I thought you wanted to be the first railway engine to go all the way around the world?" says Ace.

"That doesn't matter now," replies Thomas. "**I've got something important to do.** Good luck in the rally, Ace."

When Thomas reaches San Francisco, he is disappointed to find out that he's missed Nia.

"She's gone to China," says Amy. "I guess she wanted to be super helpful someplace else!"

Thomas asks a crane to load him on a ship to China straight away. **"I'm trying to catch up with someone,"** peeps Thomas.

"Must be a good friend," replies the crane.

"Yes, she is," replies Thomas, and he sings sadly:

"I'm sorry, so sorry. And as soon as I see you, that's exactly what I'm going to say. I'm sorry. I hope you're still my friend. **I'm sorry, so sorry, my friend."**

Thomas is now travelling through the Chinese countryside, pulling passenger coaches, but he is still missing Nia.

When he pulls into a platform, he spots Yong Bao, who he met at the Great Railway Show.

"What are you doing in China, Thomas?" asks Yong Bao.

"I'm looking for a friend from Africa," replies Thomas.

"I met a steam engine from Africa this morning!" says Yong Bao. She was heading for the Rainbow Mountains."

Now Thomas' face lights up and he races off past Yong Bao. But when he reaches the mountains, **he's sad to find that Nia is nowhere in sight.**

Heavy snow is falling as Thomas continues up into the mountains, but he finally spots Nia in the distance!

"**I'm sorry, Nia!**" peeps Thomas. "I didn't want to play a trick on you. It was Ace's idea!"

"And that makes it alright, does it?" replies Nia, hurrying ahead.

"No … because I went along with it," blushes Thomas, awkwardly. **"NIA! PLEASE! I'M SORRY!"**

But his shouts are followed by the rumbling of the snow, and Nia's wheels spin on the icy tracks as she sees the **avalanche**! Thomas tries his best to help her, but they both slide backwards, faster and faster, until they hear a voice … **It's Yong Bao with a snow plough!**

"Hold on! I've got you!" he cries as he pushes them to safety. The engines are relieved that Yong Bao came to their rescue.

"**Back to Sodor!**" cries Nia. "And then you'll be the first engine to go around the world!"

"And you will be the second!" peeps Thomas, happily.

As they travel through Europe, they sing: "**We're friends! We're friends! That's what we are. We're friends!**"

When they come to Vicarstown Bridge, Thomas stops.

"On the other side of that bridge is Sodor, and then **I'll be home**, but I guess that means you'll have to go home too."

"That's not so easy for me, Thomas," replies Nia. "The shed I used to live in isn't even there anymore."

"But that means you can **stay on Sodor with me** and all my friends!" says Thomas. "I just need to speak to The Fat Controller. **He loves having new engines!**"

But in another part of the world, The Fat Controller is still looking for Thomas, unaware he'll find him back in Sodor!

THE END